+
P656g

Guys from Space

Daniel Pinkwater

Macmillan Publishing Company   New York

Printed and bound in Japan. First American Edition 10 9 8 7 6 5 4 3 2 1

The text of this book is set in 13 point Criterion Book.
The illustrations are rendered in color markers on paper.

Library of Congress Cataloging-in-Publication Data. Pinkwater, Daniel Manus, date. Guys from Space. Summary: A boy accompanies some guys from space on a visit to another planet, where they discover such incredibly amazing things as talking rocks and root beer with ice cream.
[1. Extraterrestrial beings – Fiction. 2. Science fiction. 3. Humorous stories] I. Title.
PZ7.P6335Gu 1989   [E]   88-13485
ISBN 0-02-774672-0

To Charles, a cat,
even though he threw up
on my computer printer

I was in the backyard.
I wasn't doing anything.
There was something in the sky.
I looked up.
There was something big up there.
It was not a bird.
It was not an airplane.
It was not a balloon.
It was not a cloud.
It was something from space.
It was neat!
It was coming down.
It was coming down into the yard!
It did not make a noise.
It landed like a dream.
"This is good!" I said.
I was not scared.

When the thing from space had landed, a little door opened.

Guys from space came out.

They were no bigger than me.

"Is this Chicago?" they asked me.

"This is my yard," I said.

The guys from space talked to each other.

"Kid, would you like to come for a ride?"

"No!" I said.

"You don't want to come?"

"No."

"It will be fun," the space guys said. "We will bring you back."

"Nothing doing," I said.

"You will be the first Earth person to ride in our spaceship," they said.

"I am not allowed to go with anybody," I said. "Unless my mother or father says I can."

"Are your mother and father the same size as you?" the guys from space asked.

"Bigger," I said.

"Then they will not fit. Just you come."

"I have to ask my mother," I said.

"Is she scary?" the space guys wanted to know.

"Not very."

"All right, ask her. Where is she?"

"She's in the house," I said. "Wait here."

I went inside the house.

My mother was in the basement.

She was weaving.

She weaves.

She was weaving some sort of rug.

She has this loom.

It's what you weave on.

"There are some space guys in the yard," I said.

"That's nice," my mother said.

"Is it all right if I go up in the spaceship?"

"Sure," my mother said.

"Do you want to see the space guys?"

"Not right now, dear," my mother said. "I'm just doing the hard part of this rug."

"Then I can just go with them?"

"If you aren't late for supper."

"I'll see you later," I said.

"Have a good time," my mother said.

I went out into the yard.

"She says I can go," I said.

"Good!" the guys from space said. "Get your space helmet."

"I don't have one," I said.

"No space helmet? That's too bad."

"Don't you have an extra one?" I asked.

"Afraid not."

"Then I can't go?"

"Well, you have to have a space helmet."

"Oh," I said.

"Maybe we could fix something up. What's that?"

"That's the dog's water bowl," I said.

"What's that stuff in it?"

"Water," I said.

"Could you dump it out?" they asked.

"I guess so," I said. "Would that work as a space helmet?"

"Try it on," the space guys said.

I tried it on. "It's cold," I said. "How does it look?"
"It looks good," the space guys said. "Come on."
"Why do I have to wear this?" I asked.
"You have to. It's a rule. Let's go."
We went through the little door.
The space guys turned knobs.
They pushed buttons.
They switched switches.
Something buzzed.
Something beeped.
Something whistled.

"Here we go," the space guys said. "Look out the window."
I looked out the window.
We were going up.
"Isn't this neat?" the space guys said.
We were going fast.

"Where are we going?" I asked.

"We will visit some other planet," the space guys said.

"Will I be home in time for supper?" I asked.

"What time is supper?"

"Six."

"Easy."

"I thought other planets were far away," I said.

"They are."

"How can we go to another planet and be back by six?"

"Easy. We go fast. Hold on."

The spaceship went faster.

It went very fast.

It went very very fast.

It went faster than sound.

It went faster than light.

I didn't like it.

"This is too fast," I said.

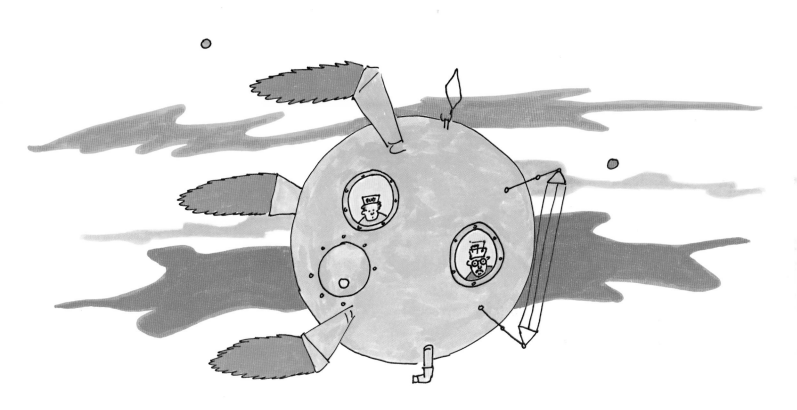

"Never mind. We have come to a planet," the space guys said.

"What planet is this?" I asked.

"Who knows? Some planet," the guys from space said. "Let's get out and look around."

"How do you know if there is air on this planet?" I asked.

"If there is no air, you can't breathe," the space guys said.

"Then what?" I asked.

"Then we run back into the spaceship and close the door," the guys from space said.

"How about wild animals and bad people?" I asked.

"Same thing. We run back inside."

"It sounds simple."

"We are space guys. We know what we are doing."

The space guys opened the door, and we went outside.

"The air is good," the space guys said.

"I don't see any wild animals," I said.

"No, this is a good planet. We can tell," the space guys said.

"What do we do now?" I asked.

"We look around. We explore."

We looked around.

It was a neat planet.

There were a lot of rocks.

I picked one up.

"Put me down!" the rock said.

I put it down.

"The rock talked," I said.

"Hello, rock," the space guys said. "We like your planet."

"Who are you?" the rock asked.

"We are guys from space," the space guys said. "We are just visiting."

"Oh, that's all right," the rock said. "Look around and have a nice time."

"Thank you," the space guys said. "Is there anything special here? Something we should see?"

"There is a root beer stand," the rock said.

"Oh, good! We like root beer," the space guys said.

"Do you like root beer?" they asked me.

"Sure," I said.

"Where is the root beer stand?" they asked the rock.

"It is there, behind that big rock," the rock said.

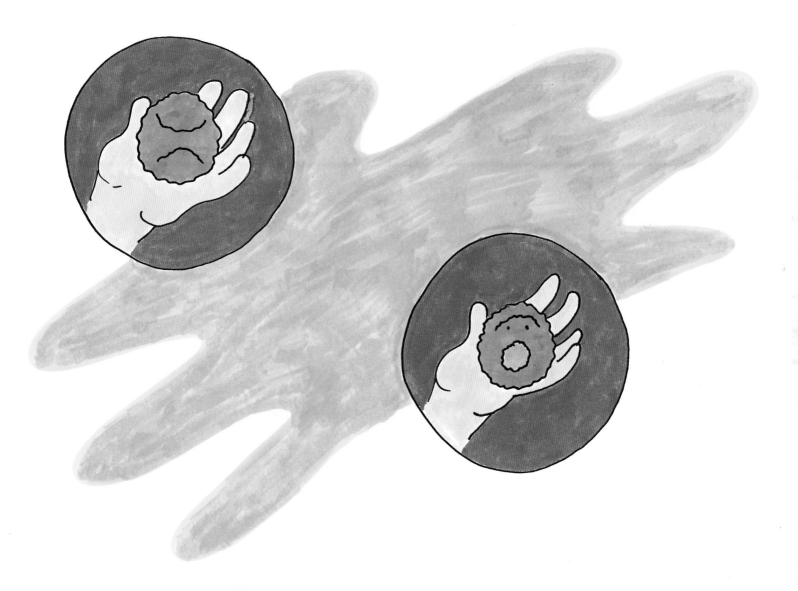

We went to the root beer stand.

It was nice.

It had lots of lights.

Space things were drinking root beer.

There was a big space thing in the root beer stand.

He was ugly, in a nice way.

"Five root beers, please," the guys from space said.

"You have money?" the big space thing said.

"We have plastic fish," the space guys said. "We use plastic fish for money."

"Plastic fish are fine," the big space thing said. "Five root beers for five plastic fish."

"On our planet, we get ten root beers for five plastic fish," the space guys said.

"Do you get ice cream in the root beers?" the big space thing asked.

"No. We never heard of ice cream in root beer," the space guys said.

"Five plastic fish for five root beers with ice cream," the big space thing said.

The space guys gave the big space thing five plastic fish.

"Ice cream in root beer," they said. "What a strange idea!"

The big space thing gave us the root beers with ice cream.

"This is good," the space guys said. "We will teach the people on our own planet about this."

I drank my root beer.

I ate the ice cream with a spoon.

I looked at the space things having root beer.

It was good root beer.

"Hurry and finish," the space guys said.

"We have to go?" I asked.

"We want to go to our own planet. We want to tell our people about ice cream in root beer. We want to go back and tell them before someone else does."

"You will take me home first?" I said.

"Yes. Now finish your root beer and ice cream."

I finished my root beer and ice cream.

We got into the spaceship.

The space guys took me home.

We landed in the backyard.

"Do you want to come in?" I asked the space guys. "Do you want to meet my mother?"

"Not now," the space guys said. "We want to go home. We want to tell our people."

"You want to tell them about root beer and ice cream."

"Yes! Our people will like it. We will be heroes."

"Thank you for the ride, and the root beer," I said.

"You are welcome," the space guys said.

"Good-bye."

"Good-bye."

The spaceship took off.

I went into the house.

"Why do you have the dog's water bowl on your head?" my mother asked.

"I used it for a space helmet," I said.

"Fill it with water and put it back," my mother said. "The dog may want a drink. Then wash your hands and face and come to supper."

"I took a ride in a spaceship," I said.

"That's nice, dear," my mother said. "Did you have a good time?"

"The space guys bought me a root beer," I said.

"I hope you thanked them," my mother said.

"I did," I said.